Halloween Magic

Troll
GLOW
IN THE
DARK

by Rita Walsh
illustrated by Steve Henry

Troll Associates

*Just hold each page
of this book under a
bright light. Then
turn out the lights
and watch it glow!*

It was Halloween, and all over the neighborhood, children were racing from house to house trick-or-treating. Everybody was having a great time.

Except for Max.

"I wish I had some friends to trick-or-treat with," said Max sadly. He had just moved onto the block, and he didn't know any of the other children.

"You'll make new friends, honey," said his mother. "Why, look, here come some children about your age right now."

Max peeked out the window and saw a group of trick-or-treaters walking to his door.

"Maybe you could introduce yourself to them," his mother continued.

Max suddenly felt very shy. He ran past his mother and up the stairs.

Max ran all the way up to the attic, slamming the door behind him. He could hear the children shouting "Trick-or-treat!" at his front door. He heard his mother calling his name.

Max sat down on the dusty attic floor. The attic was packed with lots of old boxes and trunks.

Max went over to one of the trunks and lifted the lid. Spiders scurried away as he wiped a cobweb off a heavy book.

"Magic Potions and Spells," Max read. He began turning the pages. "Wow! There are spells for everything in here!"

Max stopped at one of the pages.

Then Max had an idea. "I know," he said. "I'll use this magic spell to make a friend for myself!"

Max cleared his throat. He looked at the mysterious book and began to read aloud:

"Listen witches, hear my chant.
Don't you tell me that you can't.
A friend, a friend is what I need—
So send me one at tip-top speed!"

Max shivered. The attic began to glow with an eerie light.

Suddenly there was a tremendous BOOM! The attic door burst open and a shadowy creature rose up in the dark!

"Help! Help!" Max screamed. He ran out the door and down the steps as fast as he could.

Max's mother was standing at the front door giving
out treats. "Run!" cried Max. "There's a monster coming!"
He could hear the creature panting right behind him.

The monster chased Max out the door. "Wait for us!" cried the trick-or-treaters.

Suddenly Max tripped and fell over a crack in the sidewalk. He closed his eyes tightly as he waited for the monster to get him.

"Are you okay?" asked a friendly voice.

Max opened his eyes. All the trick-or-treaters were reaching down to help him up.

"What happened to the monster?" Max asked.

"Do you mean me?" asked a boy. He pulled off a monster mask and stepped forward. "I just wanted to invite you to come trick-or-treating with us. Your mom told me you were up in the attic. Would you like to join us?"

"Sure!" said Max. "I'll go in and put on my costume."

Max headed to his house. "I guess that old spell worked after all!" he said with a smile.